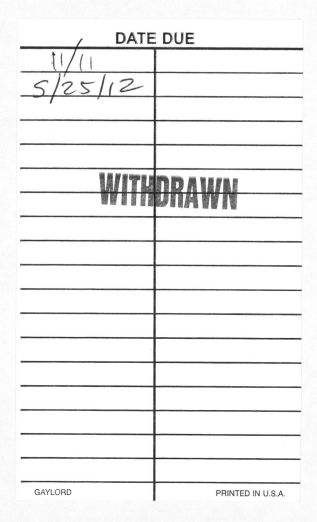

DATE DUE	
11/11	
5/25/12	
WITHDRAWN	
GAYLORD	PRINTED IN U.S.A.

THE ODIOUS OGRE

STORY BY
NORTON JUSTER
PICTURES BY
JULES FEIFFER

MICHAEL DI CAPUA BOOKS • SCHOLASTIC

For Howard and Muriel • N.J.   For Ginny and Roger • J.F.

Text copyright © 2010 by Norton Juster   Pictures copyright © 2010 by Jules Feiffer
Library of Congress control number: 2009932556   Printed in Singapore 46
Designed by Steve Scott   First edition, 2010   Third printing, 2010

There was once an Ogre who had a terrible reputation.
Not that Ogres usually have good reputations, but his was
worse than anyone could remember—or cared to remember.

He was, it was widely believed, extraordinarily large, exceedingly ugly, unusually angry, constantly hungry, and absolutely merciless.

At least, that's what everyone thought, or supposed, or had heard from someone else, or read somewhere, or had it on good authority from the grocer's wife's nephew. Nobody, however, could claim to know anything about him for sure. To tell the truth, there wasn't anyone to be found who had actually made his acquaintance and was still around to talk about it.

As it was, the very thought of him was simply too frightening to think about. And for anyone who might accidentally get close enough to see him stalking through the countryside, indescribable misfortunes were indescribed.

The one thing everyone did know for sure was that they could not think of anything to do about him.

As you can imagine, no Ogre ever had it so good.

Every time there was even a hint that he was in the neighborhood, people stuffed their ears with stale cake, blindfolded themselves, clutched their knees, and rolled up in a ball under the kitchen table.

Since this is not the most effective defensive posture, the Ogre would wander through the town, making a leisurely buffet of the local population. His every appearance increased his fearful reputation, for all that was left after each unfortunate visit was a contented smile on the Ogre's unseen face.

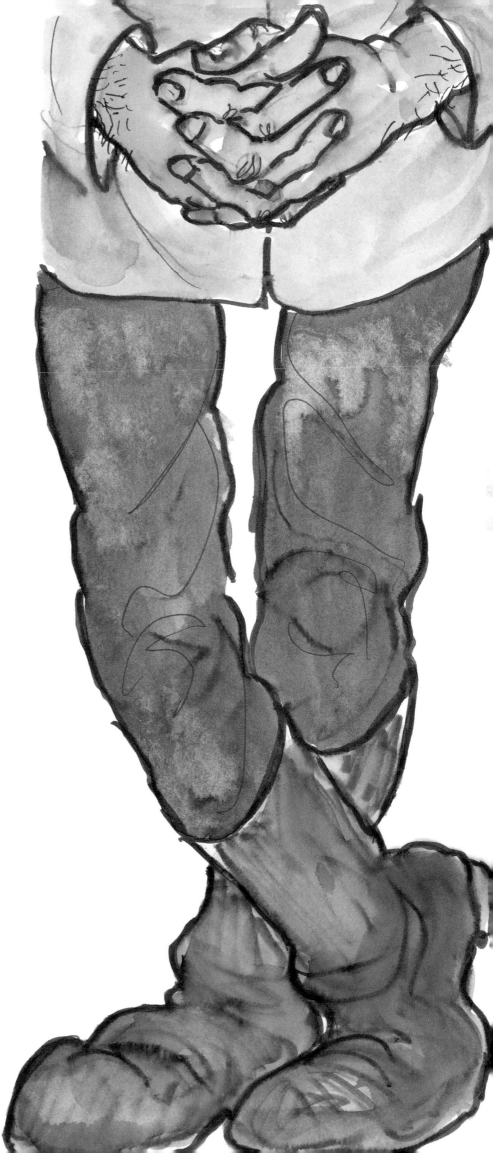

So the days passed, uneventfully for him and unhappily for the towns and villages that nestled apprehensively in the countryside. For the Ogre, it was quite a relaxing life and, as happens, he grew a bit lazy and self-satisfied, maybe even smug, and definitely spoiled. Everything came so easily for him. He grew to expect it—and to count on it.

"No one can resist me," he had to admit. "I am invulnerable, impregnable, insuperable, indefatigable, insurmountable." He let each satisfying word roll smoothly off his tongue. The Ogre did have quite an impressive vocabulary, due mainly to having inadvertently swallowed a large dictionary while consuming the head librarian in one of the nearby towns.

"What can they do? No one can resist me." He sighed and leaned back to take his morning nap.

That's the way it was for him. No doubts, no concerns, no worries. "I am invincible," he would assure himself, and then to make absolutely sure, "Absolutely invincible!"

One afternoon, as he ambled down the road towards one of the
nearby villages in search of dinner, he saw a small cottage way off
in the distance that he had not noticed before.

"Maybe I'll stop for a little snack first," he grunted,
and then lurched down the long narrow track to see what
tasty tidbit he might find.

It was a longer walk than he expected. The cottage was deep
in the woods, far removed from the busy goings-on of the world,
and unknown to the Ogre, his reputation had not preceded him.

When he finally arrived, he was dusty, tired, and even more
irritable than usual. He paused at the edge of the trees.

The cottage was quite pretty; flowers grew around the door
and there was a small orchard to one side. Even the Ogre, who
didn't care much for pretty (it doesn't taste any better than ugly),
was impressed. Then he remembered why he had come.

Outside the cottage a young girl worked busily in the garden.
She hadn't noticed the Ogre's approach.

"This is just too easy," he thought, with the slightest hint of disappointment. But as the most celebrated Ogre in the countryside, he did feel obliged to be terrifying.

So he stomped his enormous feet and roared his unbearable roar.

The trees swayed to the ground. The birds flew off in
great confusion, and even the very substantial cottage
seemed to shudder. He licked his lips.

"Oh, pardon me," the girl said softly, not looking up.
"I didn't realize anyone was there. I'll be right with you."

The Ogre looked startled. His face turned slightly pale,
his mouth dropped slightly open, and even his hands began
to tremble—slightly. "What's going on!" he mumbled.
"Why didn't she just shrivel up and collapse?" He stood
there, not sure what to do. "How dare she treat me this way!"

The girl paused in her weeding. She looked up and smiled.
"What a nice strong voice you have," she said sweetly. "But do
forgive my bad manners. Please sit down and have a cup of tea.
We get so few visitors these days."

A look of dismay crossed the Ogre's face like a sudden storm. He sat down, tentatively, on the garden bench.

"But how can you be so calm?" he sputtered. "Don't you know how terrible I am? Haven't you heard about me? Where have you been, for goodness' sake?" Suddenly she didn't seem so helpless.

"Oh, you're not really so terrible," the girl insisted, with a lovely, musical laugh. "Overbearing perhaps, arrogant for sure, somewhat self-important, a little too mean and violent, I'm afraid, and a bit messy. Your shoes could certainly use a polishing, but I'll bet if you brushed your teeth, combed your hair, found some new clothes, and totally changed your attitude you'd be quite nice."

"While you're at it," she thought to herself, "a bath wouldn't hurt either," but she was much too polite to say that.

The Ogre was now in real distress. His head felt all funny. He just didn't understand what was happening. This was not the docile dumpling he had expected.

"She hasn't even heard of me," he gasped, "and not only isn't she afraid of me, I think she likes me! I can't be liked. It's bad for business."

"One lump or two?" she inquired. "It's so nice of you to drop by. Are you new to the neighborhood?"

"NEW! I'm the scourge of the countryside. Your worst nightmare," he bellowed, trying to regain some confidence, but he didn't sound very convincing. "This is humiliating," he whimpered, "so depressing, so unfair, so embarrassing." He began to look around nervously. His eyes darted wildly from the house, to the orchard, to the forest.

The girl smiled patiently while the Ogre became more and more unnerved and fearful.

"Maybe it's a trap," he thought. "It must be a trap. YES, IT'S A TRAP!" The thought startled him. "She probably has everyone hiding in the bushes, waiting to swoop down on me. I don't much like fighting," he had to admit. "I prefer frightening. I like it when they give up."

"Look at her!" His alarm grew with every word. "She's so confident. If I pounce, she probably knows all kinds of secret, painful ways to stop me." He staggered to his feet and started to back away slowly. "What can I do? How can I live if I can't ravage and plunder?"

"I think I should be leaving," he moaned, not knowing which way
to turn.

"Oh, please don't leave before you've had a muffin," she offered
kindly. "I baked them myself this morning. They're still warm."

"A muffin! I don't want a muffin," he sobbed. "Muffins are nice,
but couldn't I have surrender?"

For the briefest of moments, his thoughts flashed back to delicious memories from his reprehensible life. But only for a moment, for his problem still stood facing him, generously offering her muffins, which he had to admit did smell good.

"This is not the way it's supposed to be," he wailed. He was sure of that, but what to do?

Then suddenly he thought he knew.

And in a last desperate attempt to reassert his fearsome presence, he drew himself up to his most menacing height, his eyes slits of determination. He leaped up and hurled himself around the garden—bellowing, stomping, blustering, grimacing, twitching, snorting, belching, clawing, and drooling, all directed at subduing the startled girl.

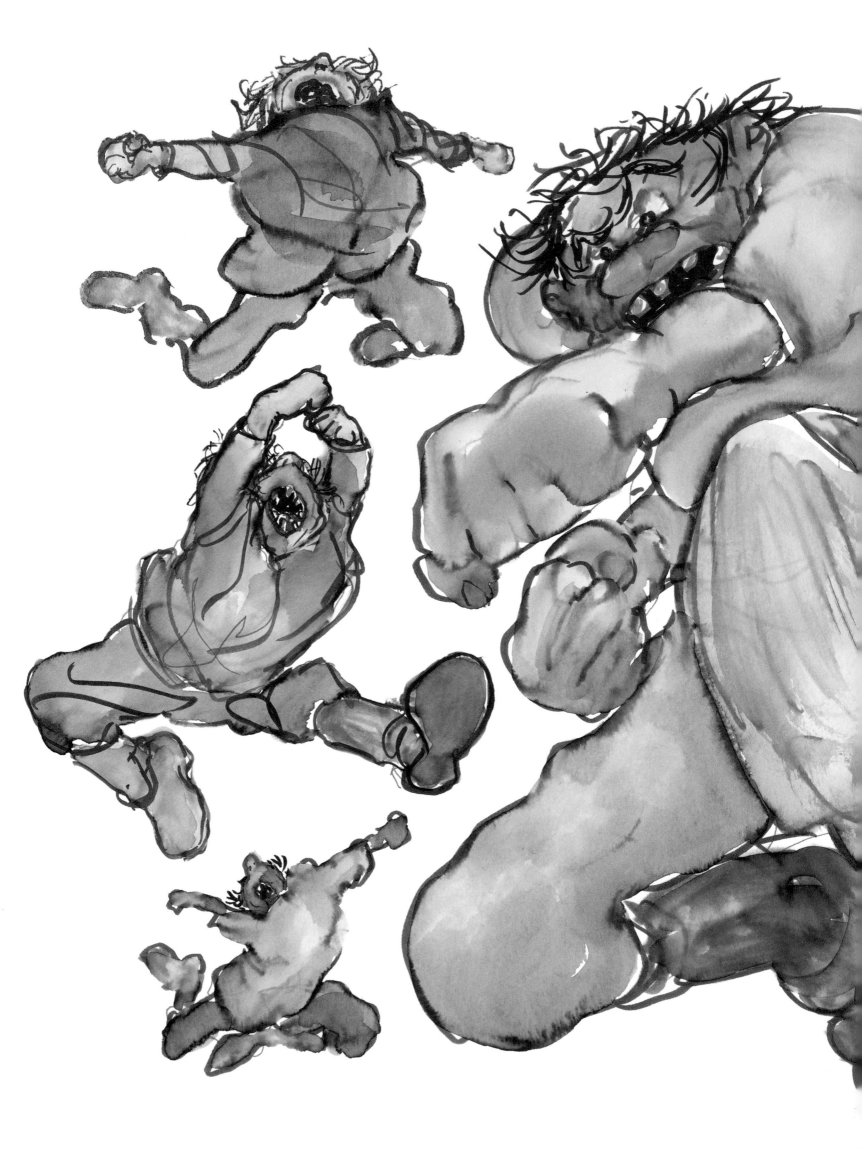

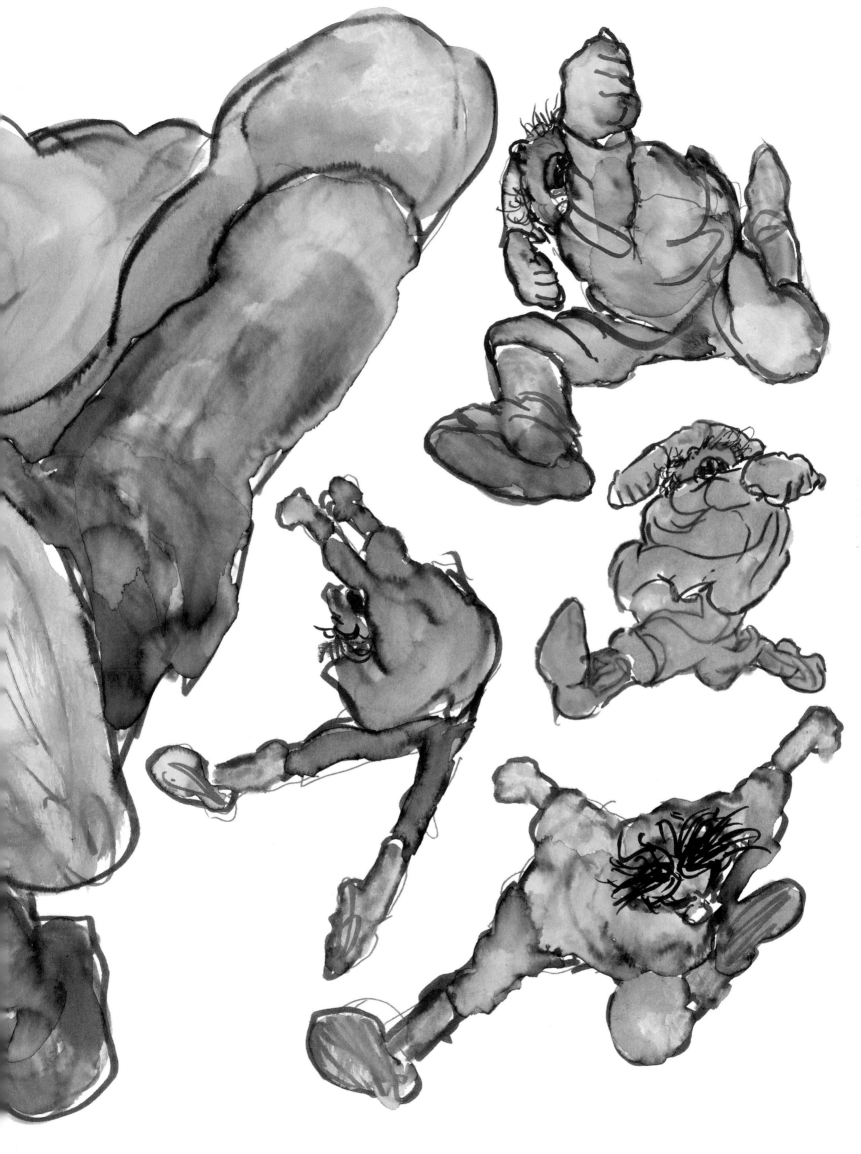

When he finished, he stood back exhausted, awaiting her abject surrender.

The girl was overwhelmed. She took a deep breath, put the muffins down carefully, and applauded with great enthusiasm for a full minute.

"What fun, how magical, how wonderful!" she exclaimed.
"Would you consider doing that for the orphans' picnic next
week? I know the children would love it."

The Ogre was stunned. Despair reached to the depths of
his shallow soul and he sagged into the tall sycamore that
stood to one side of the garden. "It's no use, I'm confounded,
overcome, and undone."

He turned and, without a word, began to walk back towards the trees, the scent of the warm muffins still lingering in the air.

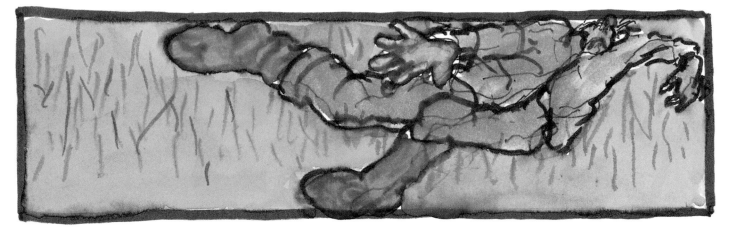

He had taken only a few steps when he stopped, stood perfectly still
for several long seconds, then stumbled back . . .

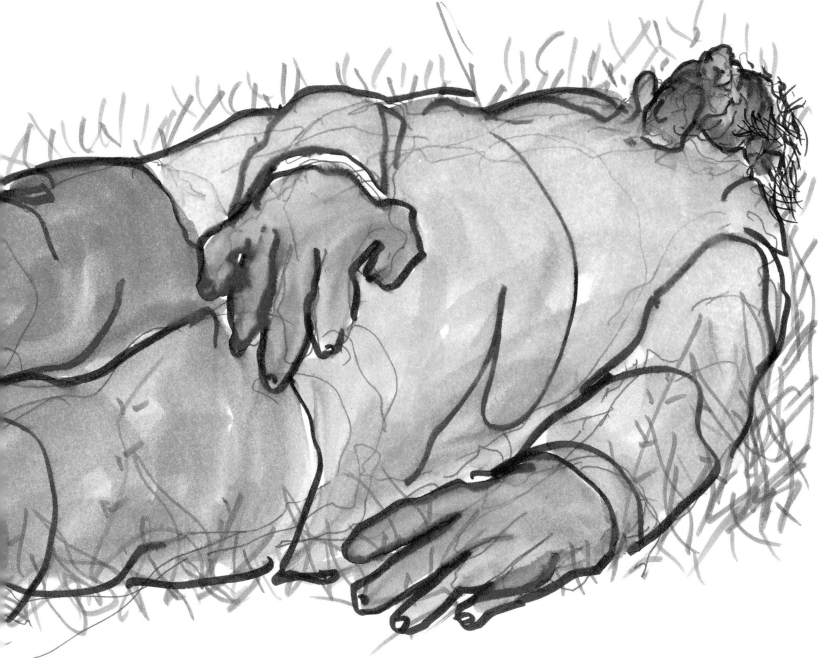

. . . keeled over, and expired on the spot, a look of
uncomprehending disbelief covering his anguished face.

When the townspeople heard the news, they all arrived to celebrate and to bury him. But most of them would not dare look at him, since reputations, of course, die harder than Ogres.

As you might expect, some of the less gracious among them were reluctant to give the girl any credit at all.

None of that mattered to the girl. It wasn't even clear to her what all the fuss was about. She had simply treated the Ogre as she treated everyone else, with kindness, generosity, and understanding.

This was just too frightening for the Ogre to bear.

She also understood that the terrible things that
can happen when you come face-to-face with an Ogre
can sometimes happen to the Ogre and not to you.